LIFE CYCLE OF A
SHARK

By Kirsty Holmes

KidHaven
PUBLISHING

LIFE
CYCLES

Words that look like **this** can be found in the glossary on page 24.

Published in 2019 by
KidHaven Publishing, an Imprint of Greenhaven Publishing, LLC
353 3rd Avenue, Suite 255, New York, NY 10010

© 2019 Booklife Publishing

This edition is published by arrangement with Booklife Publishing.

Designer: Daniel Scase
Editor: Holly Duhig

Cataloging-in-Publication Data

Names: Holmes, Kirsty.
Title: Life cycle of a shark / Kirsty Holmes.
Description: New York : KidHaven Publishing, 2019. | Series: Life cycles | Includes glossary and index.
Identifiers: ISBN 9781534526402 (pbk.) | 9781534526396 (library bound) | ISBN 9781534526419 (6 pack) | ISBN 9781534526426 (ebook)
Subjects: LCSH: Sharks--Life cycles--Juvenile literature.
Classification: LCC QL638.9 H65 2019 | DDC 597.3--dc23

Printed in the United States of America

CPSIA compliance information: Batch # BS18KL: For further information contact Greenhaven Publishing LLC, New York, New York at 1-844-317-7404.

PHOTO CREDITS

Front Cover – stephan kerkhofs, 3DMI. 1 – stephan kerkhofs, 3DMI. 2 – Willyam Bradberry. 3 – stephan kerkhofs, Tatiana Shepeleva, ALESSANDRA BARONI, wildestanimal. 4 – Voronin76, Pressmaster, Dmitry Lobanov. 5 – Alliance, Valua Vitaly, Ruslan Guzov. 6 – Kletr. 7 – Andrey Armyagov. 8 – JoLin. 9 – Rich Carey, BMCL, Andrea Izzotti, p_saranya. 10 – Angelo Giampiccolo 11 – Joe Belanger, chonlasub woravichan, AquariusPhotography, dade72. 12 – stephan kerkhofs. 13 – Ruth Black. 14 – mbolina. 15 – Grant M Henderson, frantisekhojdysz, nicolasvoisin44, Ethan Daniels. 16 – soft_light. 17 – Sergey Uryadnikov. 18 – Evgeny Karandaev, Rashevskyi Viacheslav, Christopher Robin Smith Photography. 19 – leungchopan, Catmando 20 – Grant M Henderson. 21 – BURAPHA KONGPETCHSAK. 22 – ALESSANDRA BARONI, Shane Gross. 23 – Helmut Lechner, wildestanimal. Images are courtesy of Shutterstock.com. With thanks to Getty Images, Thinkstock Photo and iStockphoto.

Please visit our website, www.greenhavenpublishing.com. For a free color catalog of all our high-quality books, call toll free 1-844-317-7404 or fax 1-844-317-7405.

LIFE CYCLE OF A
SHARK

LIFE CYCLES

WHAT IS A LIFE CYCLE?

All living things have a life cycle.
They are all born, they all grow
bigger, and their bodies change.

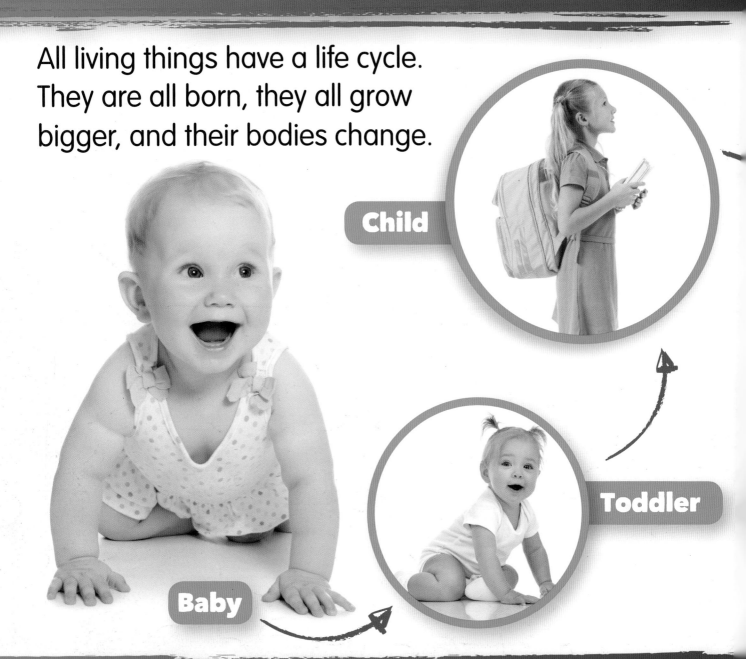

Child

Toddler

Baby

When they are fully grown, they have **offspring** of their own. In the end, all living things die. This is the life cycle.

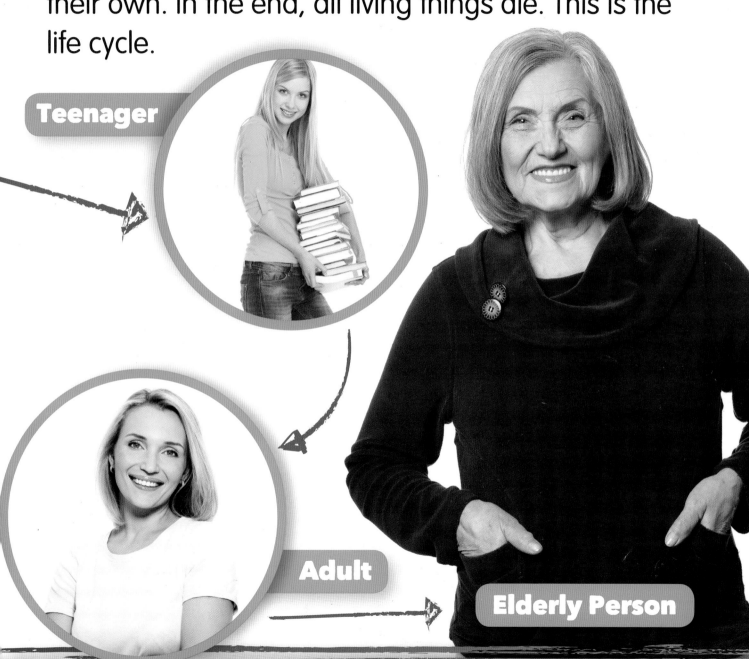

Teenager

Adult

Elderly Person

SUPER SHARKS

Sharks are a type of fish. They have long, smooth bodies, and fins and tails for swimming. They have **gills** for breathing underwater.

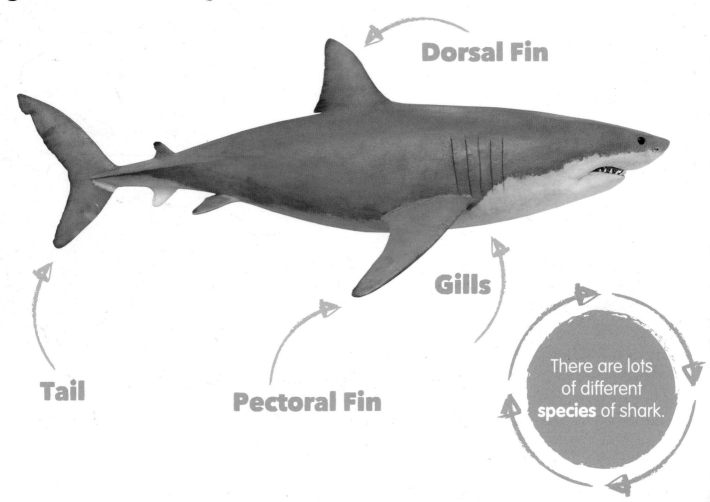

Dorsal Fin

Gills

Tail

Pectoral Fin

There are lots of different **species** of shark.

Sharks live in oceans all over the world. There are sharks in **freshwater** and ocean **habitats**, and in cold and warm areas.

EXCELLENT EGGS

Female sharks will **mate** with a male. Some females then lay eggs, but most give birth to live **young**.

Shark Egg

Shark Embryo

Shark eggs that wash up on the beach are sometimes called "mermaid's purses."

The egg contains an **embryo** which will become a baby shark. Shark eggs all look different, depending on the species they are from.

INSIDE OR OUTSIDE?

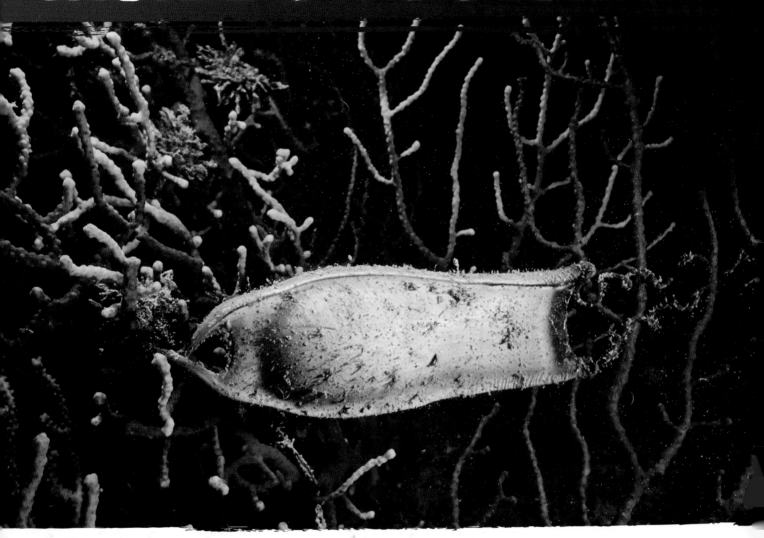

Some sharks lay their eggs in shallow water, then leave the eggs and do not return to look after their young.

Most sharks lay eggs inside their bodies.
These eggs then hatch inside the mother.
The mother then gives birth to live young.

Sharks that do this include the zebra shark, the horn shark, and the bullhead shark.

PLAYFUL PUPS

Baby sharks are called pups. Mothers do not care for their young, so pups stay together. This helps keep them safe from **predators**.

Can you spot the baby whitetip reef shark hiding in the coral?

This baby blacktip shark is hunting fish.

Because baby sharks have to look after themselves right away, they are born with teeth and can swim very well. They are just like adult sharks, only smaller.

SNAPPY SHARKS

Adult sharks have long, sleek bodies which make them good at swimming. They all have fins, gills, and tails.

Great white sharks have pointed noses – and lots of teeth!

Basking Shark

Hammerhead Shark

There are over 500 species of shark. They all look different. Some have wide faces and large, open mouths, while others have pointed noses and long faces.

Thresher Shark

Carpet Shark

LIFE AS A SHARK

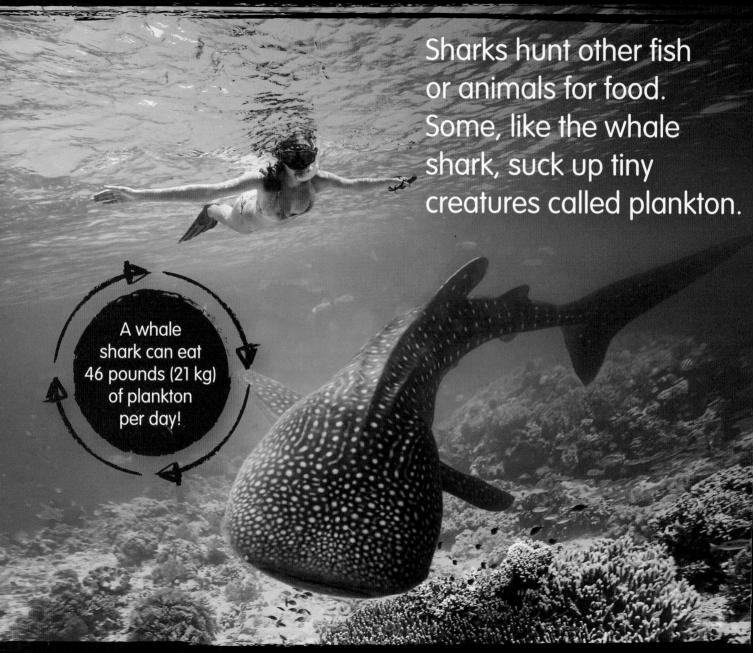

Sharks hunt other fish or animals for food. Some, like the whale shark, suck up tiny creatures called plankton.

A whale shark can eat 46 pounds (21 kg) of plankton per day!

Other sharks eat larger animals like seals or dolphins. These sharks have wide jaws and razor-sharp teeth!

Great white sharks leap from the water when hunting their **prey**.

• Sharks have been around for at least 400 million years.

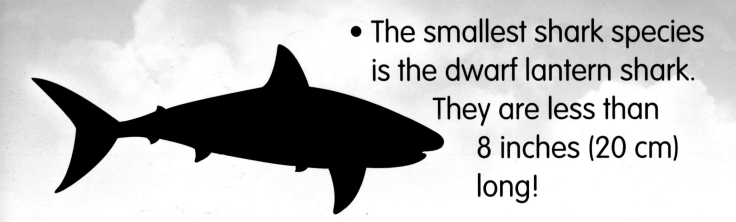

• The smallest shark species is the dwarf lantern shark. They are less than 8 inches (20 cm) long!

A shark's sense of smell is 10,000 times better than a human's.

- The largest shark alive today is the whale shark. It can grow up to 65 feet (20 m)!

- Sharks are picky eaters and will often take a bite of something before deciding whether to eat it or not!

THE END OF LIFE AS A SHARK

Most sharks live for about 20 years in the wild. However, the Greenland shark lives much longer. Some can live up to 400 years!

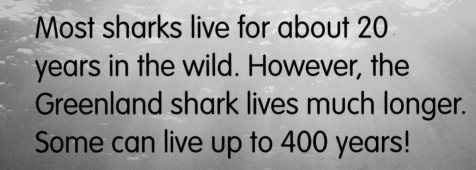

Older sharks will have lots of scars from hunting and fighting.

Sharks are at risk from **climate change**. As the waters get warmer, the fish that sharks feed on may die out. Shark **migration** will also be affected.

THE LIFE CYCLE

Egg

Pregnant Shark

The life cycle of a shark has different stages.
All the stages are different.

Shark Pup

Adult

The shark egg is laid in the water or inside the mother. The egg hatches into a pup, which looks after itself. The pup grows into an adult shark and has its own young.

In the end, the shark dies, and the life cycle is complete.

GLOSSARY

climate change	a change in the typical weather or temperature of a large area
embryo	an unborn or unhatched young in the early stages of development
freshwater	water that is not salty and doesn't come from the sea
gills	the organs that some animals use to breathe underwater
habitats	the natural environments in which animals or plants live
mate	to produce young with an animal of the same species
migration	the seasonal movement of animals from one area to another
offspring	the child, or young, of a living thing
predators	animals that hunt other animals for food
prey	animals that are hunted by other animals for food
species	a group of very similar animals or plants that are capable of producing young together
young	an animal's offspring

INDEX